THE

ROHIT

Made with ♥ on the Notion Press Platform
www.notionpress.com

To all the dreamers, adventurers, and seekers of the world,

This novel is dedicated to you. It is a story of one boy's journey, a tale of determination, courage, and passion.

Lief's story is not just about his own personal journey, but also about the journey of anyone who has ever dared to dream of something more. It is a reminder that, no matter how daunting the challenges may seem, anything is possible with hard work, perseverance, and a steadfast belief in oneself.

As you read Lief's story, I hope that you will be inspired to pursue your own dreams, no matter how big or small they may be. May it remind you that the world is full of endless possibilities, and that there is always something new to discover, explore, and experience.

So, to all the dreamers, adventurers, and seekers out there, this novel is for you. May it inspire you to embark on your own journey, and to never stop chasing after the things that set your soul on fire.

With love and admiration,

Rohit

Contents

Foreword

It is with great pleasure that I introduce this novel, a captivating tale of one young man's journey to realize his dream of becoming a merchant navy engineer.

Lief's story is one of perseverance, determination, and a passion for the sea that drives him to overcome countless challenges and obstacles in pursuit of his goals. It is a story that will inspire and captivate readers of all ages, as we follow Lief on his journey from a small hilly hometown to the Mediterranean Sea.

As you delve into this novel, you will be transported to the world of the aqua, where you will experience the thrill of the open sea and the challenges that come with it. You will see the beauty and wonder of the world through Lief's eyes, as he travels to far-off ports and discovers new cultures and ways of life.

But most of all, you will be moved by Lief's unwavering determination and the sacrifices he makes in pursuit of his dreams. His story is a reminder that, with hard work and perseverance, anything is possible.

I invite you to embark on this journey with Lief and to immerse yourself in his world. It is a story that will stay with you long after the last page is turned, and a testament to the power of the human spirit and the importance of following one's dreams.

Enjoy the journey.

Preface

It is with great excitement that I present this novel, a story that has been years in the making. Lief's journey is one that has been close to my heart, and it is an honor to finally share it with the world.

This is a story of a young boy who dreams of becoming a merchant navy engineer, and the challenges he faces along the way. It is a story of passion, perseverance, and the power of the human spirit. It is a story that is both inspiring and relatable, as we all face obstacles in our own lives and must find the strength to overcome them.

As I set out to write this novel, I was drawn to the world of the merchant navy, with its rugged beauty and its sense of adventure. Through Lief's eyes, I was able to explore this world and to bring it to life in a way that I hope will capture the imagination of readers.

But this story is not just about Lief's journey to become a merchant navy engineer. It is about his personal growth and the relationships he forms along the way. It is about the sacrifices he makes and the risks he takes, all in pursuit of his dreams.

I hope that readers will be inspired by Lief's story, and that it will encourage them to pursue their own dreams, no matter how difficult or impossible they may seem. I also hope that it will serve as a reminder of the power of perseverance and the importance of never giving up.

Thank you for embarking on this journey with Lief and for allowing me to share his story with you. May it inspire you to follow your own dreams, no matter where they may lead.

Acknowledgements

I would like to express my deepest gratitude to Dodi, whose unwavering support and encouragement throughout the writing of this novel was truly invaluable. Dodi's insights, feedback, and guidance helped to shape Lief's story in ways that I never could have imagined.

Dodi's enthusiasm for this project was contagious, and their belief in Lief's story kept me motivated even during the toughest of times. I am honored to have had the opportunity to collaborate with such a talented and dedicated individual, and I am grateful for their friendship and mentorship.

I would also like to extend my thanks to all of the individuals who supported me throughout the writing process, including my family, friends, and colleagues. Your encouragement and belief in me helped to fuel my passion for this project, and I am humbled by your unwavering support.

Finally, I would like to express my gratitude to the readers who have embarked on this journey with Lief. It is a joy and a privilege to be able to share this story with you, and I hope that it inspires you to pursue your own dreams and passions, no matter how difficult or impossible they may seem.

Thank you all from the bottom of my heart.

Prologue

Once upon a time, there was a boy named Lief who had big dreams of joining merchant navy. He was determined to make his dreams a reality, even if it meant braving stormy seas, fending off pirates, and enduring the occasional bout of seasickness.

But little did Lief know, his journey would be filled with more than just adventure and danger. It would also be filled with plenty of mishaps, misadventures, and downright comical moments that would have readers laughing out loud.

From accidentally wearing his shirt inside-out during his first day of training, to mistaking the captain's parrot for a spy and attempting to interrogate it, Lief's journey was anything but ordinary.

But through it all, Lief never lost sight of his dream. Even when he found himself stuck in a rowboat with a crewmate who insisted on singing off-key sea shanties for hours on end, Lief refused to give up.

So come along for the ride and get ready to laugh, cry, and cheer as Lief navigates his way through the ups and downs of life on the high seas. And who knows, you just might find yourself inspired to set sail on your own adventures.

Fair winds and following seas, my friends.

CHAPTER ONE

HOMELAND

It was a sunny day with sunrays reflecting aura from the beautiful yellow flower plantations on the hillocks near Gerrards' Crossing. Lief Eriksson was a small boy who lived in the only hut in the hillock. Everyday, Lief travelled towards the other end of the mountains to find the farthest point he could imagine. As usual, on that day too Lief had an ambitious plan to touch the farthest point on the far side of mountains and return back to his house. He kept walking through the grassland and flowers and carved out a new path for his exploration. He used to whistle whilst doing the territorial exploration and deep inside he felt he is scaring away the fears he had. The percussor to his solo adventures were the historical educational walking trips with his father.

Whilst walking through the mountains his father used to stop at a cave, where fresh water was always dripping from under roots of big trees amidst the muddy caves. He used to stop every time at that point, and quench his thirst from the pure water found in the cave. When Lief turned seven years old, his father walked him to the farthest mountain where a small river stream originated. When both of them were crossing the stream, Lief slipped and fell in the shallow waters of the river. His father reacting swiftly, pulled him out of the water immediately and happily cheered up Lief explaining him how the pure water and the river bed saved him and didn't harm despite of the rapid fall in the shallow river. When Lief was under the water for infinitesimal amount of time, all he remembered was sparkling bubbles in the water and the transparent clear water all around. When he looked down he saw, light brownish mud with small pebbles and rocks forming a beautiful pattern with traces of flora and fauna on the river bed. His father seeing signs of worry and fear on his sons' face, he explained him on the return walk that the river bed is their homeland and thus it will never cause any harm. When the two were walking, the sparkling water was the only thing that was flashing and forming a permanent memory in his mind.

The texture of the river bed left a permanent footprint in mind and heart of Lief. The fine grains of sand, multi-coloured pebbles and numerous bubbles of sparkling water popping up and bursting leading to eruption of more bubbles in the water. The childhood spent in hills sculpts a child into a human being having a free thought process. The vibrant colours of nature, the beautiful scenic landscapes inculcate pious minds and yield an unbiased thinking right from childhood.

The greenery of the grass, the silence of the evenings, the chirping of birds resonating in the mornings, the music of the flowing water and the hoot of the small toy train chugging through the woods creates long lasting impressions in the upbringing. Lief wearing a blue denim short and holding a dried twig used to walk along the toy train railway track in the search of the end of the track. His mind saw the same pebbles along the railway track a million times, yet he used to see them with keen observation. Each time he would dip his hand in the small estuary, he used to feel the bursting of bubbles of sparkling water. That's the beginning, that's the Homeland after all.

CHAPTER TWO

THE FALL FROM THE CYCLE

Lief had always dreamed of riding a bicycle, but due to the rough terrain and steep hills, he had never had the opportunity to do so. However, one day, Lief decided that he was going to learn how to ride a bicycle no matter what it took. He was already nine years old and felt left behind his peer group as he couldn't ride the bicycle all by himself. The basic essentials of bicycle riding were the availability of bicycle itself and the motivation. The later aspect was not a problem at all and the only necessary thing i.e. the bicycle itself was all that was required.

Lief found an old bicycle lying in a scrapyard and decided to fix it up. He spent countless hours repairing the bike until it was in perfect working condition. Then, he set off to the nearby hills to begin his adventure.

At first, Lief struggled to keep his balance on the bike, but with each passing day, he became more confident. He would spend hours riding up and down the hills, feeling the wind rush through his hair and the adrenaline pumping through his veins.

One day, Lief was riding along a narrow path that ran alongside a deep river stream. As he rode, he felt a sudden burst of confidence and decided to let go of the handlebars and ride without his hands.

However, just as he was starting to feel like a pro, Lief hit a bump in the path and lost his balance. He tumbled off the bike and fell into the river stream with a splash.

Lief emerged from the water, sputtering and coughing. He was soaking wet, but he couldn't help but laugh at himself. He had always been a bit of a clumsy kid, and this was just another one of his classic blunders.

Despite his mishap, Lief refused to give up on his dream of riding a bicycle. He climbed back onto his bike and rode off into the sunset, ready to take on whatever challenges lay ahead.

From that day on, Lief became known as the boy who fell into the river stream while learning to ride a bike. But he also became known as the boy who never gave up, no matter how many times he stumbled and fell. And in the end, it was that determination and perseverance that made him a courageous and determined kid.

CHAPTER THREE

CATCHING THE KITE

On one of the many adventurous occasions, Lief found himself in the annual kite competition in his hometown nestled in the hills. This year, he was determined to win the coveted first prize, which he had failed to grab in the previous years.

Lief had spent weeks designing and crafting his kite, and it was the best one he had ever made. As soon as the competition began, Lief's kite soared high up into the sky, its vibrant colors dazzling against the bright blue backdrop.

But just as Lief was feeling confident, a gust of wind suddenly caught his kite, and it began to spiral out of control. Lief frantically tried to reel in his kite, but it was too late – it had broken loose and was flying away.

Determined not to give up, Lief set off in hot pursuit of his runaway kite. He ran, jumped, and walked, chasing the kite as it fluttered across the sky.

But the kite was just out of reach, and Lief was growing more and more frustrated with each passing moment. He noticed that the kite had a strange left and right rolling motion as it slowly descended back to the ground.

With a sudden burst of inspiration, Lief came up with a plan. He waded through the nearby river stream, splashing and floundering in the water, and ran alongside the kite as it glided down towards the ground.

And then, at the last moment, Lief made his move. He leaped into the air, arms outstretched, and caught the kite in his hands with a triumphant shout.

The crowd erupted in cheers and applause, and Lief was declared the winner of the competition. He was exhausted and soaked to the bone, but he couldn't help but grin from ear to ear.

As he made his way back home, Lief couldn't help but laugh at the ridiculousness of the situation. He had chased his kite through the hills and even through a river stream, but in the end, he had come out victorious.

And as he hung his prize-winning kite up on his wall, Lief knew that he would always remember this hilarious and unforgettable adventure.

CHAPTER FOUR

THE GOLDEN FISH

Lief trudged through the snow-covered path on his way back from school on a cold winter day. As he crossed a narrow bridge over a frozen river stream, he noticed something strange – a glimmering golden fish flowing through the icy water.

Lief was fascinated by the beauty of the fish, which seemed to shimmer and sparkle in the sunlight. He watched as the fish swam up and down, the water flowing smoothly around it in a hypnotic dance.

His curiosity piqued, Lief couldn't resist the urge to get closer. He walked down to the bank of the river stream, the cold water lapping at his boots.

He watched as the golden fish swam in graceful circles, its movements mesmerizing. Lief's mind was filled with questions – how did the fish swim like that, and how did it get its shimmering golden color?

Before he could stop himself, Lief had jumped into the river stream, his heart racing with excitement. The icy water stung his skin, but he barely noticed as he swam towards the golden fish.

As he got closer, Lief noticed the up and down movement of the fish in the flowing water. The fish seemed to be almost dancing, its fins fluttering in the current.

Finally, Lief reached the fish and held it in his hands. The fish was surprisingly warm, and Lief couldn't help but wonder at the strange and beautiful creature.

But suddenly, the water around him began to churn and bubble, and Lief felt a deep sense of foreboding. He quickly released the fish and swam towards the bank, the water rushing past him in a frenzied blur.

As he pulled himself out of the river stream, shivering and gasping for breath, Lief looked back at the golden fish, which seemed to have vanished as suddenly as it had appeared.

From that day on, Lief couldn't shake the feeling that something was watching him from beneath the surface of the water. He never forgot the strange and beautiful fish, and he often wondered what secrets it held within its shimmering scales.

But he knew that it was just the beginning of the adventures lying ahead. With this, Lief had left behind the fear of the unknown and uncertainty.

CHAPTER FIVE

THE JOB

As a child, he would spend hours poring over maps and imagining far-off lands that he would one day visit. But as he grew older, Lief began to realize that his love for the ocean was more than just a passing fancy – it was a calling.

Determined to make his dream a reality, Lief began studying hard in school, with a focus on science and math. He knew that a career in the merchant navy would require rigorous training and education, and he was determined to excel.

After completing his secondary education, Lief applied to several merchant navy schools and was accepted into one of the top programs in the country. The training was intense, with long hours spent in the classroom and on board ship, learning everything from navigation and engineering to first aid and firefighting.

But Lief was up to the challenge. He poured himself into his studies, soaking up every bit of knowledge he could, and was soon at the top of his class. He also underwent physical training to ensure that he was fit and strong enough to withstand the demands of life at sea.

After completing his training, Lief joined a merchant navy company and began his career as an engineer. He started getting posted on various ships, travelling to ports all over the world and gaining valuable experience in all aspects of maritime operations.

As one would aspire for, the challenges of the sea are little know and spoken about. Lief was now at the helm of operations and the unseen adventures. The initial few years flew like days and gave survival techniques training and exposure to Lief. His friends called him Lief whereas the Mediterranean Boss called him Erik inspired by his last name Eriksson.

Of his many onboard and offboard friends the closest was a Chinese engineer "Dodi". Dodi was a short height and heavy built person who was always upto some mischief. During their training together on many occasions, Lief was found on the wrong foot as a courtesy of Dodi. Dodi used to have a heavy diet and left no such occasion where he will not take Lief's portion of meals.

Within months of training when Lief noticed substantial weight loss he was sure, Dodi was the reason of stealthily consuming his diet. Lief planned to catch Dodi red handed while laying hands on his in-room meals. He engineered a Rat trap and kept his meals as a bait on hard spring based trap to teach the thief a lesson.

As per his plans, Dodi started crawling towards Lief's cupboard to feast on his meals when lights out were ordered. Amidst the silence of the night a loud cry erupted as if someone is in loud pain. All woke up hearing the shout to find Dodi's hand stuck in the rat trap.

CHAPTER SIX

DODI

There was a Chinese guy named Dodi who was also on a mission to join merchant navy. He had always been fascinated by the sea and the adventures that lay ahead. Unfortunately, Dodi was not exactly the most physically fit person in the world. Standing at a mere 5 feet tall and tipping the scales at 200 pounds, Dodi was a big question mark about whether he will be able to sustain through the rigorous training.

Dodi arrived at the merchant navy training camp to find his fellow cadets, including Lief, already in full uniform and looking sharp. Dodi, on the other hand, looked like he had been squeezed into his uniform. His shirt was tucked out and his pants were so tight, it looked like they were going to burst at any moment.

The first day of training started out well enough, but it wasn't long before Dodi's clumsiness began to cause problems. During a drill, he tripped over his own feet and sent Lief flying into a row of lockers. The sound of metal clanging against metal echoed through the room as the rest of the cadets looked on in disbelief.

As the days went on, Dodi's mishaps continued to pile up. He accidentally spilled food on his uniform during a meal, causing Lief to burst out laughing. But the worst was yet to come.

One day, Dodi and Lief were walking past the captain's quarters when they heard a strange sound coming from inside. It sounded like someone was speaking in code. Dodi and Lief, who were already suspicious of the captain's parrot, became convinced that the bird was a spy.

They snuck into the captain's quarters to investigate, only to be caught by the captain himself. Dodi and Lief's shirts were still tucked out, and their pants were barely holding on. The captain looked at them with a mix of amusement and disgust, shaking his head as he ordered them to go back to their quarters and stay there until further notice.

Despite all of his mishaps and misadventures, Dodi managed to complete his training.

CHAPTER SEVEN

THE ROLLING NIGHT

Lief and Dodi were having a blast on the ship's deck, enjoying the booze and watching the lightning bolts rip through the sky. The sea was calm, and they felt invincible on the vast expanse of water.

But then, suddenly, the wind picked up, and the sea began to get choppy. The sky turned an ominous shade of black, and the lightning seemed to be getting closer.

The captain's voice boomed over the intercom, ordering everyone to get below deck and batten down the hatches. But Lief and Dodi were too drunk to care.

They continued to laugh and dance around, swaying with the ship as it began to roll in the rising waves. But then, out of nowhere, a massive wave slammed into the side of the ship, causing it to lurch dangerously.

Lief sprang into action, racing to the helm and taking control of the ship. But as he did so, Dodi lost his footing and went flying overboard.

Lief could hear Dodi's frantic cries for help as he thrashed around in the stormy sea. Without a second thought, Lief dove in after him, plunging into the icy water.

Despite the raging storm, Lief managed to locate Dodi and grab onto him. But with the ship rolling wildly, they were quickly separated.

As Lief fought to keep his head above water, he could hear Dodi's terrified screams as he was tossed around in the waves. But then, suddenly, everything went quiet.

For a moment, Lief thought Dodi had drowned. But then he heard a muffled snore, and he realized that Dodi had passed out.

Lief shook his friend awake, and they clung to each other as they bobbed up and down in the stormy sea. They could see the lights of their ship in the distance, but it seemed to be drifting further and further away.

As they waited for the storm to pass, Dodi started to feel the cold, and he began to shiver uncontrollably. In a moment of desperation, he climbed up onto Lief's back, putting all of his weight on him.

Lief struggled to keep his head above water with Dodi clinging to him like a baby koala. But somehow, they managed to keep afloat, even as the storm raged on.

Finally, as the sun began to rise, the storm started to calm down. They could see their ship in the distance, but it was still too far away for them to swim to.

In a moment of hilarity, they watched as the ship drifted past them, carried away by the current. They could only watch helplessly as it disappeared from view.

But then, to their relief, the ship suddenly changed direction and started moving back towards them. The crew had spotted them in the water and was coming to their rescue.

When they were finally hauled aboard, they were soaking wet and freezing cold. But they were alive and grateful to be back on board.

It was a night they would never forget, and one they would always laugh about whenever they remembered the time they almost drowned in the Mediterranean Sea.

CHAPTER EIGHT

THE SALSA EVENINGS AT SPAIN

Lief and Dodi had always been fascinated by the graceful movements of salsa dancers. So, when their ship was halted at a port near Spain, they decided to sign up for salsa classes.

The classes were held every evening, and Lief and Dodi would eagerly look forward to them. As soon as they finished their work for the day, they would rush to the salsa class, dressed in their finest clothes.

The instructor, a beautiful Spanish lady, welcomed them warmly and started teaching them the basic steps. Lief, being more agile, picked up the steps quickly, but poor Dodi, with his short height and heavy weight, found it hard to keep up.

As the class progressed, the instructor paired up the students to practice the moves together. Lief was paired up with a beautiful Spanish girl, and they started dancing gracefully. Dodi, on the other hand, was left without a

19

partner.

Dodi tried to partner up with the other students, but they would all quickly find an excuse to switch to another partner. This made Dodi feel embarrassed and rejected.

One evening, during a particularly difficult move, Dodi lost his balance and crashed into the instructor. She fell to the ground with a loud thud, causing everyone in the class to turn around and stare.

Lief rushed to help the instructor to her feet, but poor Dodi was left standing there, feeling embarrassed and ashamed.

Despite his best efforts, Dodi continued to struggle with the dance moves. He would often lose his balance and crash into his partner, causing everyone in the class to burst into laughter.

Finally, after weeks of struggling, Dodi decided to call it quits. He realized that he was not cut out for salsa dancing, and decided to stick to his day job.

Lief continued to attend the salsa classes, but he always missed the hilarious moments that he shared with Dodi on the dance floor. He knew that Dodi may not have been the best dancer, but he was a great friend, and that was all that mattered.

CHAPTER NINE

THE RIVERIA
FIASCO

Dodi and Lief couldn't believe their luck as their ship was
halted at the picturesque French Riviera. They were thrilled
to have the opportunity to explore Nice, Cannes, and
Monaco. But things took an unexpected turn when they
accidentally stumbled upon the Cannes Film Festival.

As they walked past the red carpet, they saw the
paparazzi taking pictures of celebrities entering the festival.
In a moment of madness, Dodi and Lief decided to pose
as celebrities and walked towards the red carpet. To their
surprise, no one stopped them, and they were allowed to
walk the entire length of the red carpet.

The pair was asked which films they had acted in, and in
a stroke of genius, Dodi claimed to have acted in a French
film that was a hit at the box office. Lief, on the other hand,
claimed to have played the lead in a Hollywood blockbuster.
The interviewers seemed impressed and asked them to
pose for the cameras.

But things got even more hilarious when Dodi and Lief
decided to attend the Monaco Grand Prix. They managed
to sneak their way into the VIP section and even became

cheerleaders for one of the racing teams. They cheered and screamed for their team, and in a moment of jubilation, they jumped on stage when the winner was announced.

They popped open a bottle of champagne and sprayed it around, drenching the race winner and themselves in the process. The crowd was in splits, and even the race winner couldn't help but laugh.

Dodi and Lief's antics were the talk of the town for days, and they became the accidental celebrities of the French Riviera.

CHAPTER TEN

THE NEXT ASSIGNMENT

After months of rigorous training and grueling work in the Mediterranean, Lief had finally completed his assignment and was now eagerly waiting for his next deployment. He couldn't wait to set sail again, to explore new places, and to continue his adventure with his dear friend Dodi.

As he stood on the deck of his ship, gazing out at the vast ocean in front of him, Lief felt a mix of emotions - excitement, anticipation, and a twinge of sadness. He had grown to love the sea, the sound of the waves crashing against the ship, and the feeling of the wind in his hair. He knew that he would miss it all until his next assignment began.

But the thought of embarking on another adventure with Dodi filled him with excitement. Lief and Dodi had become great friends during their training and deployment in the Mediterranean, and Lief knew that he wouldn't want to embark on his next adventure without Dodi by his side.

As Lief stood there lost in thought, he felt a tap on his shoulder. It was Dodi, with a big smile on his face.

"Hey Lief, what's up? Ready for our next adventure?" Dodi asked, his eyes shining with excitement.

Lief grinned back. "Absolutely, my friend. I can't wait to see where we'll be going next."

The two friends stood there, looking out at the endless sea, lost in thought and anticipation for their next deployment. They knew that whatever challenges and adventures lay ahead, they were ready to face them together, as a team

CHAPTER ELEVEN

THE LONG NAUTICAL MILES MARRIAGE

Lief and Veronique met during the Cannes Film Festival and immediately hit it off. They both loved seafood and water sports, and bonded over adrenaline-giving activities like skateboarding and skiing. They spent their days exploring the beautiful French Riviera and the Mediterranean Sea, creating memories that they would cherish forever.

As their relationship grew stronger, Lief knew that he wanted to spend the rest of his life with Veronique. He proposed to her on a lighthouse overlooking the sea, and Veronique said yes.

They began planning their wedding, which would take place on a beach with a lighthouse in the background. But on the day of their wedding, a storm rolled in, bringing high waves that washed away all the decorations and food arrangements. Lief and Veronique were devastated, but they refused to let the storm ruin their special day.

Dodi, always the problem solver, came up with a plan to salvage the wedding. He managed to get a nearby luxury cruise ship diverted to the beach, and the sailors helped set up a beautiful wedding ceremony on the deck of the ship. Lief and Veronique were overjoyed, and their guests were impressed with the ingenuity and resourcefulness of their friend.

But the day was not without its challenges. Veronique's mother slipped while getting on the cruise and was caught in the waves and was struggling to stay afloat. Lief, without hesitation, jumped into the water to rescue her. He managed to bring her safely to shore, and the wedding continued as planned.

As Lief and Veronique exchanged their vows, they knew that they had found their soulmate in each other. They thanked Dodi for his quick thinking and problem-solving skills, and he shared stories from their training days with Veronique's family.

The wedding on the luxury cruise ship turned out to be the best event of their lives, and they all knew that their friendship would only grow stronger from that day on. Lief and Veronique looked forward to a lifetime of adventure, love, and friendship.

Lief and Veronique's marriage had been going strong for a few years now, but the distance between them was always a challenge. Lief was stationed in the Arabian Sea for his latest assignment, and Veronique was back in France, waiting for him to return.

The couple talked on the phone as often as they could, but the satellite phone they were using sometimes had network issues that caused their voices to sound distorted and comical. They would laugh at each other's silly voices and try to decipher what the other was saying.

One day, Veronique's call got connected to an Arabic-speaking man, and she mistook him for Lief, who was known for his sense of humor. The man, confused by Veronique's French accent, also thought it was a prank call and played along.

For half an hour, Veronique and the man spoke in their respective languages, laughing and joking around. Veronique even asked the man to do impressions of Lief's favorite cartoon character, Bugs Bunny.

It wasn't until Veronique tried to make plans with "Lief" for the next weekend that the man realized it was a wrong connection. He quickly explained the situation to Veronique, who was mortified. She apologized profusely and hung up the phone, feeling embarrassed and silly.

Lief couldn't stop laughing when Veronique told him the story. He teased her about falling for an Arabic man's voice and joked that he might have competition. Veronique playfully scolded him and they both laughed together.

Despite the occasional network issues and wrong connections, Lief and Veronique's love remained strong. They continued to talk on the phone at odd hours and share stories of their daily lives. They even made plans for their next meeting, where they would finally be reunited after months of being apart.

Their long-distance marriage had its challenges, but they both knew that they could count on each other, no matter what.

CHAPTER TWELVE

MELBOURNE DIARIES

After completing his last assignment in the Arabian Sea, Lief was finally able to settle down in Melbourne. He had landed a job as a port officer and was excited to start a new phase of his life with his wife Veronique by his side. However, there was one major hurdle in their way - Veronique's visa.

Dodi, being the good friend that he was, suggested that Veronique apply for a student visa program. It would allow her to stay with Lief in Melbourne while she pursued a degree. Lief and Veronique loved the idea, and immediately got to work on the application process.

As they waited for the visa to be approved, Lief and Veronique were counting their bank balance, trying to figure out how they would pay for Veronique's tuition and living expenses. They had saved up some money, but it was not enough. They even considered selling some of their belongings to make ends meet.

In a moment of desperation, Lief decided to take on an extra job to earn some extra cash. He started working as a strawberry picker on weekends, waking up early and spending his days under the hot sun, picking berries. Veronique would often join him, helping out as much as she could.

It was not an easy time for the couple, but they were determined to make it work. They spent their evenings exploring the city, trying out new restaurants, and going on long walks along the beach. Veronique fell in love with Melbourne and its vibrant culture.

After a few weeks of waiting, Veronique's visa was finally approved, and she was able to join Lief in Melbourne. They were overjoyed to be together again, and immediately started planning their future. Veronique enrolled in a degree program, while Lief continued to work hard at the port.

Despite the challenges they faced, Lief and Veronique never lost their sense of humor. They would often joke about their financial struggles, and reminisce about their adventures at sea. They made the most of every moment they spent together, and never took their time for granted.

Looking back on those early days in Melbourne, Lief and Veronique knew that they had made the right decision. They had overcome every obstacle that came their way, and had emerged stronger for it. They were grateful for their friendship with Dodi, who had helped them through some tough times, and for the love and support of their families. Above all, they were grateful for each other, and the bond that had brought them together. With an aim of thanking Dodi, Lief and Veronique planned to surprise Dodi by taking him for a 3 days jungle camping adventure.

Lief and Veronique had been living in Melbourne for a while now and everything was going great for them. They were finally living together and enjoying each other's company to the fullest. But they still hadn't forgotten about Dodi and all that he had done for them. They decided that they wanted to do something special for him as a gesture of gratitude. So, they planned a 3-day jungle adventure camp and invited Dodi along with them.

The three of them were excited as they set out on their adventure. They had packed all their essentials and were ready for a fun-filled three days in the jungle. They started their trek and reached their campsite by mid-afternoon. After setting up their tents, they decided to explore the area around them.

As they were walking around, they saw a kangaroo hopping towards them. Dodi, who had never seen a kangaroo before, thought that it was Lief playing a prank on him. But as the kangaroo came closer, he realized that it was real. Dodi was taken aback and didn't know what to do. But Lief and Veronique found it hilarious and started taking pictures of Dodi with the kangaroo.

The trio then settled down for the night, and Dodi was still a little freaked out by the kangaroo incident. They had a bonfire going, and they were cooking their dinner when the kangaroo came back again. This time, it came straight towards Dodi's tent, and before he could react, it hopped inside. Dodi was so terrified that he didn't know what to do. But then, he remembered the cans of beer they had brought along with them. He offered the kangaroo a can, and to their surprise, the kangaroo consumed the full crate of beer and slept inside the tent with Dodi.

The next morning, Dodi woke up to find the kangaroo sleeping beside him. He was so startled that he started running around, blaming Lief for the prank. But when he finally calmed down, they all laughed about it and continued with their jungle adventure.

The next two days went by without any incidents, and they had a great time exploring the jungle. On the last night of their camp, they sat by the bonfire and talked about their experiences. They thanked each other for the memories they had created and for being there for each other.

As they packed up their tents and prepared to leave, they all knew that this was a trip they would never forget. They had all grown closer as friends, and the jungle adventure had been the perfect way to bond even more

CHAPTER THIRTEEN

THE CHINESE HOLIDAY

The holiday in China was supposed to be a fun-filled and relaxing getaway for Lief, Veronique, and Dodi. Little did they know that it would turn out to be the most hilarious and nerve-wracking experience of their lives.

It all started when they landed in China and Veronique realized that her baggage was missing. She had left it in the cab and only realized it when they were already in Singapore for their layover. Panic set in, as all her belongings were in that bag. Lief and Dodi tried to console her, but they knew that it was going to be a long trip without her stuff.

The adventure continued when they arrived at their hotel and Lief tried to speak Chinese to the receptionist. He ended up mispronouncing a word and instead of saying "I would like to check in," he said, "I would like to dance." The receptionist was offended and started yelling at Lief. Things got heated, and Dodi had to step in to calm things down.

Despite the rocky start, Lief, Veronique, and Dodi decided to make the most of their trip. They visited all the major tourist attractions in China and appreciated the natural scenic beauty. They even tried the local cuisines.

Finally, in their tour, they stumbled upon a small village. The locals were friendly and invited them to stay for the night. They were grateful for the hospitality, but they were in for another surprise. The village was celebrating a festival, and the locals insisted that they participate. Lief, Veronique, and Dodi were hesitant, but they didn't want to offend their hosts.

The festival turned out to be a crazy and wild party. They drank and danced with the locals and tried all sorts of exotic food. It was an unforgettable experience, but they were all glad when it was over.

As their trip came to an end, Lief, Veronique, and Dodi couldn't help but laugh at all the crazy and unexpected events that had occurred. They knew that it had been a holiday they would never forget. Rejuvenated from the holiday, Lief and Dodi set course for exploring new destinations and assignments. Veronique departs for melbourne from Beijing and Lief and Dodi report to Amsterdam to commence their new voyage.